P9-CFM-982

CARTOON NETWORK

SCOOBY-DOO!

AND THE

SEASHORE SLIMER

Look for these recent **Scooby-Doo Mysteries.**
Collect as many as you can!

Written by
James Gelsey

A
LITTLE APPLE
PAPERBACK

SCHOLASTIC INC.
New York   Toronto   London   Auckland   Sydney
Mexico City   New Delhi   Hong Kong   Buenos Aires

If you purchased this book without a cover, you should be aware that this book is stolen property. It was reported as "unsold and destroyed" to the publisher, and neither the author nor the publisher has received any payment for this "stripped book."

No part of this publication may be reproduced in whole or in part, or stored in a retrieval system, or transmitted in any form or by any means, electronic, mechanical, photocopying, recording, or otherwise, without written permission of the publisher. For information regarding permission, write to Scholastic Inc., Attention: Permissions Department, 557 Broadway, New York, NY 10012.

ISBN 0-439-28488-0

Copyright © 2002 by Hanna-Barbera.
SCOOBY-DOO and all related characters and elements
are trademarks of and © Hanna-Barbera.
CARTOON NETWORK and logo are trademarks of and
© Cartoon Network.
(s02)
Published by Scholastic Inc. All rights reserved.
SCHOLASTIC, LITTLE APPLE, and associated logos are
trademarks and/or registered trademarks of Scholastic Inc.

Designed by Carisa Swenson

12 11 10 9 8 7 6 5   2 3 4 5 6 7/0

Special thanks to Duendes del Sur for cover and interior illustrations.
Printed in the U.S.A.
First Scholastic printing, April 2002

Chapter 1

The Mystery Machine zoomed down the winding coastal highway. On one side, Fred, Daphne, and Velma watched the waves of the ocean crash into the sandy shore. On the other, enormous sand dunes towered over the van. Suddenly, a giant shark poked its head into the front of the van.

"Whoooaaa!" shouted Fred. The van swerved a bit before Fred got it back under control.

"Shaggy! Scooby!" scolded Daphne. "Be careful with your beach toys!"

"Like, sorry, Daph, sorry, Fred," Shaggy said. "Scooby and I were just blowing up old Chompers here for the beach. But he got away from us."

"Reah, rorry," Scooby echoed.

Shaggy pulled the inflatable shark into the back of the van. Then he and Scooby poked their heads up front.

"Are we almost there?" Shaggy asked.

"Any minute now," Daphne said. "I don't know about the rest of you, but I'm really looking forward to a  nice, peaceful vacation."

"I'm curious to see Muccalucca Milt," Velma said. Shaggy and Scooby looked at each other and giggled.

"Like, mucca-who-a-what?" asked Shaggy.

"Muccalucca Milt," Velma repeated. "As in Cape Muccalucca, the town where the beach is."

"With a name like that, Scooby, he could be one of your cousins," joked Shaggy.

Scooby shook his head. "Rot ry rousin," he barked.

"I should hope not," Daphne said. "Muccalucca Milt isn't a dog. He's a pelican."

"He's the town mascot," Fred said. "Every year at this time, Muccalucca Milt takes off from his nest and flies around the town's lagoon. If he returns to his nest without stopping, that means it's going to be a short summer."

"Right," Velma said. "But if he dives for fish before returning to his nest, that means the town's going to have a long summer and a big tourist season. Muccalucca Milt hasn't been wrong yet."

"And that's, like, all he does?" asked Shaggy.

Fred, Daphne, and Velma nodded.

"What a life, huh, Scooby?" said Shaggy. "He just has to work one day a year. And the rest of the time he gets to hang out on the beach. What a lucky duck."

Scooby shook his head. "Ruh-uh," he said. "Rucky relican."

Everyone laughed as the van turned off the highway. They drove along a two-lane road toward a town in the distance. As they neared the town, the gang saw people standing along the side of the road.

"Those people look like they're carrying signs," Velma said.

Fred slowed down the van so they could read one of the signs.

"'Save the Pinkey Fish,'" read Daphne. "It looks to me like they're not going to be too happy about the Pinkey Fish Cook-off."

"Rinkey Fish?" asked Scooby.

"Pinkey Fish are a special kind of fish found only in the waters around Cape Muccalucca," Velma said. "The cook-off is a big cooking contest."

Shaggy's and Scooby's eyes lit up and their mouths dropped open.

"Like, did you say 'cooking contest'?" asked Shaggy.

Velma nodded.

"Scooby, I'm thinking that they're going to need some judges for that contest!" Shaggy said.

"And I'm thinking our vacation may not be so peaceful after all." Fred smiled.

Chapter 2

F red drove the Mystery Machine through the town and found a parking spot right next to the beach. A row of shops lined the other side of the street.

"Like, here we are, Scooby," Shaggy said. "Time to hit the beach."

Shaggy and Scooby jumped out of the van. Shaggy wore a floppy-brimmed straw hat, round sunglasses, and sandals on his feet. Scooby's flower-print swim trunks matched the flower-print towel draped around his neck.

As Fred, Daphne, and Velma climbed out of the van, an elderly couple passed by. The couple was dressed in white from head to toe. The woman carried a big straw beach bag. A green beach towel was hanging out of it.

"Look at those kids," the man said, shaking his head. "The summer hasn't even officially started and tourists are already invading the town."

"Now, Sheldon, relax," the woman said. "We don't even know how long summer's going to be yet. You wouldn't want to use up all your anger now."

"Excuse us, but we're looking for Muccalucca Milt," Daphne said.

"Well, I'm not him," the man snapped.

"Sheldon, behave yourself," his wife said. "Right over there, dear, where that crowd is gathering around the gazebo."

"Do you ever go to watch Muccalucca Milt?" asked Velma.

"We've lived here all our lives, dear," the woman answered. "We've seen Muccalucca Milt for as long as there's been a Muccalucca Milt."

"If you ask me, I wish there never was a Muccalucca Milt," Sheldon said. "He's ruined our nice, quiet little beach town. Because of him, tourists come here and fill up our restaurants, empty our grocery store, and make life plain miserable for the rest of us."

A man standing behind the couple cleared his throat. He wore white slacks, a flowered shirt, and a wide-brim hat with a fake pelican perched on top.

"Ah, Mayor Handy," Sheldon said. "Getting ready to begin the annual ruination of our town?"

"Actually, I'm getting ready to celebrate what I feel is going to be our biggest summer ever," the mayor replied.

"We'll see about that," Sheldon said. "Come on, Ida. Let's go get ready for the cook-off."

As Sheldon walked away, Ida reached into her bag and pulled out a large index card.

"He's been working all year on this recipe," Ida said. "He's sure it's going to win this time. And you know what? This time I think he's right!"

"See you later, Ida!" Mayor Handy called as Ida hurried to catch up with her husband.

"Don't let Sheldon Flagstone bother you," Mayor Handy said. "He's our official town grump. I'm Mayor Sanford Handy. Welcome to Cape Muccalucca!" He tipped his pelican hat.

"Thank you, sir," Fred said. "I'm Fred. And this is Daphne, Velma, Shaggy, and Scooby-Doo."

"You'd better hurry over to the gazebo now," Mayor Handy said. "Muccalucca Milt's about to do his thing."

"Is it true that Muccalucca Milt's never been wrong?" asked Velma.

As the mayor nodded, the bird on his hat bobbed with him.

"So how do you think he does it?" asked Fred.

"They say that animals have a sixth sense about things," the mayor answered. "I just hope that this year his sense tells him to get some fish. The past few summers have been cut short by storms, and that drives the tourists away. One more short season, and our town will be in some serious trouble. See you kids later."

Mayor Handy tipped his pelican hat again and walked away.

"Jinkies!" Velma said. "I wanted to ask the mayor about those people we passed on our way into town."

"I can tell you about them," a voice said from behind them. "They work for me."

Chapter 3

The gang turned around and saw a young woman standing there. She wore a snorkel mask on top of her head and a green towel around her neck. One of the signs the gang had seen earlier leaned against her leg.

"I'm Sassy Prentiss, and I'm the president of SOP," she said.

"What's SOP?" asked Daphne.

"It stands for 'Save Our Pinkey Fish,'" Sassy explained. "The lagoon over there is one of the only known breeding grounds of the Pinkey Fish. We're trying to save them from becoming extinct."

"Have you had any success?" asked Velma.

Sassy shook her head. "Not really," she said. "It's hard with all the tourists who flock here. So far only the old folks who hate the tourists have signed our petitions. No one really cares about the Pinkey Fish."

"Ah, but there you are mistaken," a man said as he walked by.

The gang glanced over and saw a man dressed in a green-and-black-striped beach robe. He wore black sandals on his feet, a green towel around his neck, black sunglasses, and a wide-brimmed green hat with a black band around it.

"I, for one, care greatly about the Pinkey Fish," the man continued.

"You do?" asked Sassy.

"Absolutely," the man said. "I care whether they are broiled or fried. Whether they're in chowder or bisque. Whether they're —"

"Stop it! Stop it!" Sassy cried as she covered her ears. "You're horrible! You and everyone else in this town! Someone ought to teach all of you a lesson!" Sassy grabbed her bag and ran away across the beach.

The man peered out over the top of his sunglasses.

"I would say she can't take a joke," he said with a smile. "Only I wasn't joking. Roger Clarksinton, at your service. You may not know me, but I'll bet you know my restaurants."

Roger spun around and showed the gang the back of his beach robe.

"Hey, that's the skull and crossbones on pirate flags," Fred said.

"That's me," Roger said, turning back around. "Jolly Roger Clarksinton."

"As in Jolly Roger's Seafood Bonanza?" asked Velma.

"One and the same," he answered.

Shaggy and Scooby licked their lips.

"Like, we love Jolly Roger's," Shaggy said. "Especially the all-you-can-eat buffet."

"So what brings you to Cape Muccalucca, Mr. Clarksinton?" asked Fred.

"Please, call me Jolly Roger," he said. As he spoke, he removed his sunglasses and polished them with a green handkerchief. Velma noticed a skull and crossbones embroidered into the fabric.

"I'm entering one of my secret seafood recipes in the Pinkey Fish contest," he said, pulling an index card from his pocket. A recipe was written on it. "And when it wins, I'm going to use the publicity to help me launch a national chain of Jolly Roger's Pinkey Fish Bonanzas."

"Sounds like you'll need a lot of Pinkey Fish for your restaurants," Daphne said.

"Yes, and isn't this the perfect place to grow them?" he said, looking around. "It's well known that the waters around Cape Muccalucca produce most of the country's Pinkey Fish. And there are people across the nation who have never even tasted Pinkey Fish. It's a crime."

The crowd on the beach was growing larger.

"Excuse me, Jolly Roger, but I think it's almost time to see Muccalucca Milt," Fred said.

"Have a good time," Jolly Roger said.

"Come on, gang!" Fred said.

Chapter 4

The gang walked across the sand and joined the crowd gathered around the gazebo. Many of the people wore pelican hats just like the mayor's.

"What's the big deal about a gazebo?" asked Shaggy.

"It's not the gazebo, Shaggy, it's what's on top," Daphne said. "Muccalucca Milt's nest."

Velma pointed to a box sitting on the very top of the white structure. Twigs and leaves drooped over the sides. Shaggy and Scooby could barely make out a white shape poking out of the top.

"He's waking up!" cried someone in the crowd.

Everyone gazed at the nest. Muccalucca Milt raised his head and yawned with his enormous beak.

"Zoinks!" Shaggy exclaimed. "I'll bet he could fit an entire slice of pizza in his mouth at once."

"Ror a role rizza rie," Scooby added.

The pelican stretched out his white feathered wings. He flapped them a couple of times and then drew them back against his body. He appeared to be looking down at the crowd beneath him.

"This is when he's supposed to take off and get some fish," Fred said.

"Or not," Velma said. "We won't know until he does it."

A few minutes passed and the crowd continued to watch and wait.

"Like, I don't know about you guys, but standing out in this hot sun is making Scooby and me feel like french fries," Shaggy complained.

"Reah, rench ries," Scooby echoed. He used his towel to wipe his forehead.

"Hmmm, speaking of french fries . . ." Shaggy began. His gaze turned to the snack bar just down the beach.

"Oh, no, you don't," Daphne said. "We came here to see Muccalucca Milt, not to snack our way down the beach."

"But Daph," Shaggy protested, "me and Scoob haven't eaten anything since . . . since . . ." Shaggy tried to remember the last time they ate. Then it hit him. "Since breakfast! We're going to starve to death if we don't eat something soon."

Before Daphne could answer, Mayor Handy shouted, "He's getting ready to fly! He's getting ready to fly!"

Muccalucca Milt spread his wings, raised his head, and lifted off from his nest. The large bird flew up into the air and around the lagoon two or three times. Then, just as Muccalucca Milt started diving toward the water, a piercing shriek filled the air. The pelican pulled up and circled around the lagoon again. Soon everyone heard another shriek.

"It sounds like it's coming from the stage on the other side of the lagoon," Fred said.

"Take it easy, everyone," Mayor Handy announced. "Probably just a kid having some fun. I'll take care of it."

As Mayor Handy walked toward the stage, a hideous sea monster jumped out at him. The creature had the head of a fish and a body that trailed long strands of sea slime.

"CREEEEEEEEEEEEEEEEE!" it screamed. Its bright-green, clawlike hands snapped at the air.

The crowd shrieked in dismay. Everyone was frozen where they stood.

"Rikes!" shouted Scooby.

"Zoinks!" cried Shaggy at the same time.

They each tried to jump into the other's arms but collided in midair and crashed to the ground.

Meanwhile, the creature shrieked again and ran down the beach. It slimed the mayor and then ran toward the lagoon.

"It's going after Muccalucca Milt!" Daphne cried.

They watched helplessly as the sea monster ran beneath the flying pelican. It raised its claws and snapped at the air. Muccalucca Milt flapped harder and flew away, out over the ocean.

"Come back, Milt!" the people called.

The monster turn back toward the crowd at the gazebo.

"CREEEEEE!" it screeched.

People ran from the beach screaming, jumping into their cars or hiding in the beachfront shops. The sea monster ran back to the stage and ripped apart the 'PINKEY FISH COOK-OFF' banner with its claws. Then it jumped to the ground and disappeared into the tall grass behind the stage.

"This is terrible!" moaned Mayor Handy as he wiped the monster's green gunk from his arms and legs. "Muccalucca Milt's gone, and there's a slimy sea monster running around. Our town is doomed!"

"Don't worry, Mr. Mayor," Fred said. "You take care of finding Muccalucca Milt. Mystery, Inc. will take care of everything else."

Chapter 5

"**C**ome on, gang, let's get to work," Fred said. He led the others across the beach to the Pinkey Fish Cook-off stage.

"Since this is where the monster came from and returned to, this is where we're going to start looking for clues," Fred said.

"I have a better idea," Shaggy said. "Since this is where the monster came from and returned to, how about we get out of here?"

"Reah!" said Scooby. "Routta rere!"

"We promised Mayor Handy we'd help solve this mystery," Velma said. "Besides, if we don't try to find the monster, then they're going to have to close the beach."

"Including the snack bars and the Pinkey-Fish Cook-off," Daphne added knowingly.

"In that case, what are we waiting for?" asked Shaggy. "You go first, Scooby." Shaggy gave Scooby a nudge toward the tall grass behind the stage.

"I'll go back there with Shaggy and Scooby," Velma said.

"Good idea, Velma," Fred agreed. "Daphne and I will look around the front of the stage."

Shaggy and Scooby followed Velma behind the stage. They faced a wall of saw grass almost as tall as them.

"Man, this is the tallest grass I've ever seen," Shaggy said. "Looks like someone hasn't mowed it in years."

"This kind of saw grass can grow up to seven feet tall," Velma said. "But be careful of its edges. It's called saw grass for a reason."

Velma noticed two different spots where the grass appeared to be trampled.

"I'll bet the sea monster used these two paths," Velma guessed. "One when it came out and one when it ran away. I have a hunch either one of them will lead us right to it. Let's split up to make sure. I'll take the path on the left. You two take the one on the right."

Velma quickly disappeared into the tall grass, leaving Shaggy and Scooby behind.

"All right, Scooby, the quicker we get this over with, the sooner it'll be snack time," Shaggy said. "So let's go."

Shaggy and Scooby followed the path of trampled grass. As the tall blades of grass waved in the wind, they brushed against Scooby's fur. He started giggling.

"Re-he-he-he-he-he-he."

"What's so funny, Scooby?" asked Shaggy.

"Ruh rass rickles," he said.

"All right, pal, one super Scooby back scratch, coming up," Shaggy said.

"Roh, roy!" barked Scooby. He stood on all fours as Shaggy cracked his knuckles and reached down and scratched Scooby's back from neck to tail.

"How was that, Scoob?" asked Shaggy.

"Rerrific!" Scooby answered. He gave Shaggy a lick.

"You're welcome, old buddy," Shaggy replied. "Now let's find the end of this trail so we can get out of this creepy overgrown lawn."

As they started walking again, they heard a rustling sound in the grass. Then Shaggy saw a flash of something green whiz by.

"Zoinks!" Shaggy gulped. "Did you see that?"

"Ruh-uh," Scooby answered. "Rhat ras rit?"

"Something fast and green," Shaggy answered. "Like the big green claws on that slimy sea monster. Let's get out of here, Scoob!"

Shaggy and Scooby turned and ran back down the path. Shaggy peered over his shoulder and caught another glimpse of the green thing.

"Hurry, Scoob!" Shaggy shouted. "It's getting closer!"

They ran with all their might through the tall saw grass.

"Coming through!" yelled Shaggy. He and Scooby burst through the grass and crashed right into Fred and Daphne. All four of them fell to the ground.

"Shaggy! Scooby! What's going on?" Fred asked.

"Like, we saw that monster's grabby green claws snapping through the grass," Shaggy answered, out of breath. "He was right behind us and almost grabbed us, too."

"You mean like this?" asked Velma from behind. Her left hand was wrapped in a green beach towel. She reached out and grabbed Shaggy's shoulder with it.

"Aaaaahhhh!" cried Shaggy.

Fred, Daphne, and Scooby laughed as Velma unwrapped the towel.

"It was only me, Shaggy," Velma said. "I was right about that path. It led to a clearing where I found this towel with some of the creature's slime on it." She held up the green towel.

"Like, why would a sea monster need a beach towel?" asked Shaggy.

"An excellent question, Shaggy," Velma said. "But we're going to need to find more than a towel to answer it."

"Maybe I can help," someone said from the stage.

Chapter 6

The gang walked around to the front of the stage and saw Jolly Roger Clarksinton standing there. He had changed from his beach clothes into baggy green-and-black pants and a black shirt. Velma noticed the skull and crossbones embroidered on his pocket.

"I was just getting something from my yacht over at the dock," he said. "Mayor Handy was there organizing a search party for that pelican. Anyway, he told me you were trying to find the sea monster."

"That's right," Fred said. "But so far, we haven't had much luck."

Roger looked around and then motioned for the gang to get closer. They climbed onto the stage and gathered around him.

"Well, I was on my yacht when the whole thing happened," Roger whispered. "A few moments after I heard all the commotion, I saw someone run out of the saw grass."

"Really? Who?" asked Daphne.

"I couldn't tell," Roger said. "But it looked like they were carrying a large paddle of some kind."

"Like you'd use to paddle a boat?" asked Fred.

"Or maybe like you'd use to protest something," Velma said. "I'll bet it was really one of SOP's signs. It only looked like a paddle because it was so far away."

"Hmm, Velma could be right," Fred said. "Thanks, Jolly Roger. You've been a big help."

"My pleasure," he replied. "I've got to check on my pot of Pinkey Fish Surprise now. It's simmering on the stove in my yacht. Good luck finding the monster. And stay clear of those nasty claws of his." With a smile and a wave, Roger Clarksinton jumped off the stage and headed back to the dock.

"Come on, gang, let's see if we can find Sassy Prentiss," Fred said.

As the gang prepared to climb down, Velma noticed something on the floor of the stage. It was partly concealed by the banner the sea creature had destroyed.

"Hmm, that's odd," she said.

"What is it?" asked Fred.

Velma picked up a white index card and handed it to Fred.

"'Pinkey Fish Surprise,'" he read. "Hey, this looks like someone's recipe for the cook-off."

"It was covered by a piece of the banner the sea creature cut up," Velma said. "It must have dropped it when it was up here onstage."

"You mean the sea monster wanted to enter the cook-off?" asked Shaggy.

"Shaggy, it didn't want to enter the contest," Daphne said. "At least not as the sea monster."

Fred and Velma nodded.

"Daphne's right," Fred said. "With this next clue, we're getting much closer to figuring out who's really behind this whole mess. But I say we still try to find Sassy Prentiss."

"I'm with you, Fred," Velma said. "Let's go."

"Okay, you three have fun," Shaggy called. "Scooby and I will hang out here,

NOT using any of the cooking tools."

"All right, we'll catch up with you later," Fred said. Fred, Daphne, and Velma climbed down and walked across the beach.

"Okay, they're gone, Scooby," Shaggy said. "Now let's have some fun."

Shaggy picked up a chef's hat and put it on. Scooby grabbed a frying pan and a spatula.

"Welcome to *Cooking with Shaggy*," Shaggy said in a funny French accent. "Today's special will be Scooby Surprise."

Scooby dropped the spatula. As he turned around to pick it up, he came face-to-face with the slimy sea serpent!

"Rikes!" he cried.

"Relax, Scooby," Shaggy said. "Scooby Surprise is just the name of the dish. You don't really have to act surprised." Shaggy turned to smile at Scooby — and saw the sea monster.

"CREEEEE!" shrieked the monster. It sliced Shaggy's chef's hat in half with its giant green claws.

"Let's get out of here!" cried Shaggy. He and Scooby leaped off the stage with the sea monster right behind them.

Chapter 7

The giant sea monster chased Shaggy and Scooby off the stage and onto the beach. It reached down and grabbed a clawful of slime from its belly and flung it through the air.

SPLAT! The slime hit Shaggy on the back of the head.

"I've been slimed! I've been slimed!" Shaggy cried. He ran straight for the lagoon and dived in. Scooby followed as Shaggy swam out to the middle of the lagoon. The two of them thrashed around in the water, desperate to get away from the monster.

"Help! Help!" yelled Shaggy. "The monster!"

Mayor Handy and a few others ran onto the beach. They saw Shaggy and Scooby in the middle of the lagoon, splashing around.

"Stand up, Shaggy," the mayor called.

"What?" Shaggy replied.

The mayor and the other people then shouted together, "Stand up!"

Shaggy stopped thrashing. He slowly lowered his feet and felt the sandy bottom of the lagoon. He stood up and found that the water only came up to his chest. Scooby stood up, too.

"Like, thanks, man!" Shaggy called to the others.

"You can come out now," Mayor Handy said.

"Not until that sea monster is gone," Shaggy replied.

"What sea monster?" asked the mayor.

Shaggy and Scooby looked around. There was no sign of the slimy monster that had chased them just moments before.

"Uh, never mind," Shaggy said. He and Scooby slowly walked through the water to the beach. As they came out of the lagoon, Fred and Velma ran over.

"Are you two all right?" Velma asked. "What happened?"

"Sounds like these two were chased by the sea monster," Mayor Handy said.

"We were on the cooking stage when all of a sudden the thing appeared and almost grabbed us in its shiny green claws," Shaggy said.

"Reah, rike ris," Scooby added. He reached out with one of his front paws and snapped at Mayor Handy's nose.

"Sounds like you two could use a break," Daphne said. She walked over and handed Shaggy a paper plate full of french fries.

"You're a lifesaver, Daph," Shaggy said.

"Reah, ranks, Raphne," Scooby echoed. Scooby took a handful of fries and stuffed them into his mouth.

"Where are your manners, Scooby?" asked Shaggy. He took a small lobster fork from his front pocket and stabbed two french fries with it.

"Shaggy, what are you doing?" asked Daphne.

"Eating," Shaggy answered.

"Where did you get that fork?" asked Fred.

"Oh, this?" Shaggy said. "I just found it in the sand."

"May I see that?" asked Velma.

Shaggy shrugged and handed the tiny lobster fork to Velma. She examined it closely and then handed it to Fred.

"The sea monster must have dropped this while chasing Scooby and Shaggy," Velma said.

"Judging by the design," Fred said, "I'd say this is no ordinary lobster fork."

"And no ordinary clue," Daphne added.

"If you ask me, I'd say it's time to make sure our slimy sea monster goes out with the tide," Velma said.

Fred nodded. "Velma's right. It's time to set a trap."

Chapter 8

"We have to make the sea monster believe that Muccalucca Milt has come back," Fred explained. "Mayor Handy, is there a fishing net we can borrow?"

"There's a whole bunch of them down by the dock," the mayor answered.

"Great," Fred said. "Shaggy and I will hide inside the gazebo with the fishing net. When the sea monster shows up, we'll snare it in the net."

"Like, what makes you so sure the monster will come over to the gazebo?" asked Shaggy.

"That's where Scooby comes in," Velma said. "Scooby will be disguised as Muccalucca Milt. He'll be sitting up in his nest."

"Rup rhere?" Scooby asked. "Ro ray!"

"That goes double for me," Shaggy said.

"That's too bad," Daphne said. "If we don't capture the monster, there won't be a cook-off. And without a cook-off, I guess they won't be needing any judges."

"Let's not be hasty, Daphne," Shaggy said. "You mean we get to judge the cook-off if we help?"

Mayor Handy smiled. "I don't see why not," he said.

"Then count me in," Shaggy said. "How about you, Scooby?"

Scooby thought for a moment, then shook his head. "Ruh-ruh," he said.

"Then how about doing it for a Scooby Snack?" asked Velma.

Scooby's eyes lit up.

"Rokay!" he barked. Daphne tossed a Scooby Snack into the air. Scooby stuck out his tongue and snatched the treat. He happily munched it down.

"Now that we've got that settled, let's get to work," Fred said. He strode toward the dock to get the net. Velma and Daphne stayed behind to help Scooby get ready.

"Mayor Handy, can we borrow your hat?" asked Daphne.

"Absolutely," he said, handing her his pelican hat. "I'll go get you kids a ladder. There's one under the stage."

Daphne put the hat on Scooby's head.

"Not bad," she said. "Can you flap your wings like a pelican?"

Scooby sat down and stretched out his front paws. He waved them up and down.

"Maybe you'd better forget about the flapping, Scoob," Shaggy said.

Fred returned with the net just as Mayor Handy came back with the ladder. They leaned the ladder against the side of the gazebo.

"Good luck, Scooby," Shaggy said.

Scooby slowly climbed up the ladder and onto the roof of the gazebo. He pulled himself into the pelican's nest and sat down.

"Now act like a pelican!" Shaggy called.

He and Fred stepped into the gazebo with the net and crouched down. Mayor Handy,

Velma, and Daphne stepped back and pointed up at the nest.

"He's here! He's here!" yelled Velma.

"Look! Muccalucca Milt has come back!" shouted Daphne.

"The summer is saved!" cried Mayor Handy.

A small crowd of people started gathering on the beach. All they could see was the top of Scooby's head, which looked just like Muccalucca Milt. Everyone cheered. Soon, a sizable crowd had formed.

Mayor Handy stood on the steps of the gazebo.

"In honor of the return of our beloved Muccalucca Milt," he proclaimed, "I hereby declare the beginning of summer — and Cape Muccalucca's tourist season!"

As the crowd cheered again, Scooby heard a screeching sound in the distance.

"Re's rack! Re's rack!" he shouted down to the others. But everyone was pretending to celebrate and couldn't hear Scooby. A moment later, the slimy sea monster ran out from behind the stage.

"CRRREEEEEE!" it shrieked. As quickly as they had gathered, the townspeople dispersed. The creature ran across the sand, snapping at the air. It headed right for the gazebo, shrieking at Scooby.

Fred and Shaggy jumped up and threw the net over the monster. The creature struggled for a bit but quickly snipped through the net with its sharp claws.

"Zoinks!" shouted Shaggy. "Let's get out of here!"

He and Fred leaped from the gazebo and ran across the beach. The monster saw the

ladder and slowly started climbing up toward Scooby.

"Relp! Raggy!" cried Scooby.

Desperate, Scooby took off his Muccalucca Milt hat and threw it at the monster. The monster waved it away with one claw and then lost its balance on the ladder. The ladder tilted back and wobbled in the air before slamming back against the gazebo again.

The ladder's impact shook Muccalucca Milt's nest. Scooby lost his balance and tumbled out of the nest. He slid down the roof and crashed into the ladder. Scooby, the sea monster, and the ladder went flying backward. The monster let go and fell to the sand. The ladder crashed down next to it. And Scooby landed right on top of the monster.

Chapter 9

Everyone ran over to Scooby and the sea creature. Shaggy and Daphne helped Scooby up while Fred and the mayor wrapped the monster in the cut-up net.

"Are you okay, Scooby?" asked Shaggy.

"Reah." Scooby nodded.

"Are you ready to see who's the real monster, Mayor Handy?" asked Fred.

"You bet," the mayor replied. He grabbed hold of the fish head and gave a mighty yank. The mask popped off. "Jolly Roger Clarksinton!"

Everyone in the crowd gasped.

"Just as we suspected," Velma said.

"You did?" asked the mayor. "How could you possibly have known?"

"It wasn't easy," Fred said.

"We met a few people who could have been suspects, and the first clue we found confirmed our suspicions," Daphne said. "It was a green towel that Velma found in the saw grass."

"We remembered that Sassy Prentiss, the Flagstones, and Jolly Roger each had a green beach towel with them," Velma explained. "And they each had a different reason for wanting to disrupt this year's tourist season."

"And what's wrong with that?" called Sheldon Flagstone from the crowd. He and Ida stepped forward. "With all the tourists taking over, this town's gone to the dogs."

Scooby cocked his head.

"Ruh?" he said.

"Sorry, no offense," Sheldon said.

"Which is one of the reasons you remained a suspect after we found the next clue," Fred said. "It was a recipe card for the Pinkey Fish Cook-off."

"Did you lose the recipe card, Ida?" Sheldon asked.

Ida rummaged through her straw bag and took out a white index card.

"Relax, Sheldon, it's right here," she said.

"But we didn't know that at the time," Daphne said. "All we knew is that both you and Jolly Roger showed us index cards with recipes on them."

"So that left the two of you as suspects," Velma said. "But then Jolly Roger tried to throw us off the trail. He said he saw someone carrying a paddle or a sign run out of the saw grass soon after the monster left the beach."

"Finally, it took a plate of french fries for us to find the last clue," Fred said. "Shaggy found a lobster fork in the sand where the monster had chased him and Scooby. The fork had a special monogram on it: Jolly Roger's skull and crossbones."

"But I could have dropped that anytime," Roger said. "That didn't prove anything."

"It proved you were on the beach where the sea monster was," Daphne said. "Even though you had told us earlier that you were on your yacht when the monster showed up."

"Interestingly, you had also warned us to stay clear of the monster's claws," Velma said. "Something you couldn't have known about if you never saw the monster."

Jolly Roger lowered his head in defeat.

"Why did you do this, Roger?" asked Mayor Handy.

"Because I needed Cape Muccalucca's waters for my Pinkey Fish farm," Roger replied. "I was going to ruin the tourist season so I could buy out the town. It was supposed to become the base of my new chain of seafood restaurants. And I was this close to doing it." He raised up one of his claws and held the pincers inches apart. "But then those kids and their meddling mutt showed up and ruined everything."

The town's police showed up and escorted Jolly Roger away.

"Look! It's Muccalucca Milt! He's really back!" shouted Ida Flagstone.

The crowd cheered as the pelican circled above them and landed in its nest. Milt opened his enormous beak and three fish jumped out.

"Three fish!" exclaimed Mayor Handy. "He's never caught three fish before. This is incredible. We may be in store for the best summer ever!" The mayor turned and looked at the gang. "And we owe it all to you and your brave dog."

Just then, Muccalucca Milt took off from his nest. He circled over the crowd, swooped down, and grabbed the mayor's pelican hat in his beak. Milt flew up into the air and slowly brought himself down over Scooby. Very carefully, he placed the hat back on Scooby's head and landed on the ground. "Raaaaawwwwk!" crowed Muccalucca Milt.

"Scooby-Dooby-Doo!" barked Scooby.

About the Author

As a boy, James Gelsey used to run home from school to watch the Scooby-Doo cartoons on television (only after finishing his homework). Today, he still enjoys watching them with his wife and two daughters. He also has a real dog named Scooby who loves nothing more than a good Scooby Snack!

COMING TO MOVIE THEATRES SUMMER 2002

AOL KEYWORD: PowerpuffGirls